The Epic Tale
of Jag-Man

The Epic Tale of Jag-Man

Patrick C. Moore

J. Kenkade
PUBLISHING®
LITTLE ROCK, ARKANSAS

J. Kenkade Publishing
6104 Forbing Rd
Little Rock, AR 72209
www. jkenkadepublishing. com
Facebook.com/jkenkadepublishing

J. Kenkade Publishing is a registered trademark.

Printed in the United States of America
ISBN 978-1-944486-92-1

SERIES VILLAINS:

Poncho Guerrow – San Antonio
Hugo "The Tank" Johnson – Chicago
Stealth Man – Los Angeles
Jim "The Punisher" Boyd – Pittsburgh
The Panther – Atlanta
Ms. Swan – Denver
Thunderbird – Tampa
The Cardinal – Boston

ACCESSORIES:

Jag-Mobile
Jag-Cycle
Jag-Helicopter
Jag-Boat
Jag-Truck
Jag-Four-wheeler
Jag-Plane

TABLE OF CONTENTS

Chapter 1: The Beginning   9
Chapter 2: Shades of Superpower   17
Chapter 3: Prom Day   27
Chapter 4: College & Draft Day   41
Chapter 5: Reunited   55
Chapter 6: Rouge Stone Valley   69
About the Author   97
About J. Kenkade Publishing   99

Chapter One
The Beginning

IT WAS MID-MORNING ON A SATURDAY when Max began an argument with his brother Robert and Robert's friends Rex, Randy, Sam, Donald, and Ed. The whole conflict was about Robert and his friends' secret cave that was supposed to be hidden in the woods behind Max and Robert's house. For months, Robert and his friends had teased Max. They said he was too small and young to go with them into the woods and play in their hideaway.

Max had finally had enough and was bound and determined to go find his brother's cave by himself. Max began his quest by first going to the kitchen and retrieving some snacks and drinks to fill his Scout backpack. Then he was off to the garage. Max was going so fast, it looked like he had ants in his pants. Once Max was in the garage, he retrieved what he believed would be the best survival gear a young ten-year-old boy his age would need to find Robert's hidden cave in the woods. By the time Max had gathered everything he needed, it was high noon.

Max saw his mother in the laundry room folding clothes. Max told her that he was going down to Cisco's house to play a little kickball and dodgeball. Max's mom was oblivious to his real intentions. For the first time, Max lost his integrity; he had lied to his mom. Lying to his mom affected Max deeply. He knew it was wrong to lie, and he knew the difference between right and wrong from a very young age. At that point, he promised himself never to lie again.

Finally, Max set out on that fabulous fall afternoon to conquer his mission. Max had been walking around in the woods for a little over two hours when he began to think he was lost and his stomach was beginning to growl with hunger. Max desperately wanted to find the perfect spot to sit down and eat his snacks. Max spotted a tree that had fallen over. It was the biggest tree Max had ever seen! That tree must have fallen over because of the record-setting ice storm Bayou Ridge County had received back in January. As Max approached the tree, he thought he heard something rustle in the leaves on the other side of it.

Unlike his brother Robert, who was the daredevil in the family, Max was pretty conservative. Before Max could say Jiminy Cricket, a jaguar leapt over the fallen tree and was staring Max in the eye. Max stood frozen in his tracks as he thought about what his next move should be. He remembered that he had made two peanut butter sandwiches earlier before he left the house. Max slowly bent down, took his backpack off his shoulder, and then gently and slowly unzipped the backpack and took out the bag with the peanut butter sandwiches. Cautiously, Max looked up to see if the jaguar was still staring at him. Sure enough, it was.

At first, Max thought his only option was to throw the sandwiches at the jaguar, but Max started to have second thoughts. Just like that, a lightbulb went off in his head: this should be the time he quit being the conservative kid. He decided to join his brother Robert as the second Rockafellor daredevil in the family. Max started slowly but surely walking toward the jaguar. Max was about halfway toward the jaguar when it let out a very loud hissing sound. Before that day, that sound would have made Max run faster than a jack rabbit back through the woods and to his house. That day was different. Max almost jumped out of his boots when the jaguar hissed at him, but overall, he was actually cool, calm, and collective. Max could feel a sense of courage run throughout his body. Max reached out to give the peanut butter sandwich to the jaguar. The jaguar bit into the sandwich just as Max let it go.

Max still felt calmness and courage, and he backed away slowly as the jaguar quickly scarfed down the peanut butter sandwich. The jaguar looked at Max and turned its head slightly to the side as if to say thank you. Max slowly did an about-face and started to walk down a different path. Max was still determined to finish his quest and find Robert's hidden cave in the woods.

A half hour had now passed, and Max had still not found his brother's hidden cave. As Max was walking through the woods, he heard the sound of giant footsteps in the leaves behind him. When Max stopped, the sound of the giant footsteps stopped. When Max started walking again, he heard the sound of the giant footsteps again.

Finally, Max yelled out, "Robert, if that's you and your friends, please stop trying to scare me and show yourself!"

There was no answer from Robert.

The woods were quiet. Then the crackling and crunching sounds of the leaves began again. They were getting louder and louder. Then *whoosh!*

The ugliest, creepiest thing that Max had ever seen suddenly appeared in front of him. It was a one quarter wolf, one quarter bear, one quarter pig, and one quarter man. While casting a giant shadow over Max, this wolf-bear-pig-man had risen up on his back paws and let out a mighty roar. To Max, the wolf-bear-pig-man looked like a giant, bearing razor sharp claws and extremely long wolf fangs.

Then, all of a sudden, the giant raised his right paw as if preparing to take a swipe at Max. Max realized he would be severely hurt if this wolf-bear-pig-man smacked him with his paw. Max was so afraid. Within a split second, the wolf-bear-pig-man's paw swiped with a burst of speed down toward Max. As this was happening, Max observed a flash of light out of the corner of his eye. He realized he had not been struck by the giant's paw. Max shut his eyes and was not sure what just happened. Max decided that the flash of light he saw was the jaguar jumping between him and the giant. Max realized the jaguar saved his life.

Max was looking at the wolf-bear-pig-man, and then he saw the jaguar. The jaguar let out a killer roar and then hissed at the wolf-bear-pig-man. The wolf-bear-pig-man seemed to be in shock and ran off into the woods.

Max glanced over to the jaguar and saw that it was hurt and in some serious pain. Max saw that the wolf-bear-pig-man had clawed the jaguar on its right shoulder. Max quickly went over and checked out the jaguar's wounds.

Max had forgotten that earlier that day he had cut his finger with a knife. He failed to put a band-aid on the open wound. He had in a rush to find Robert's hidden cave, and the cut did not seem that important to him.

As he drew closer to the jaguar, he was amazed by what he saw. Without thinking, Max reached out and gently rubbed the jaguar's wound with the hand that he had cut earlier in the morning. At that exact moment, something tremendous happened.

Upon Max's open wound and the jaguar's open wound touching, a brand-new world with a bright new future was in store for Max Rockafellor. Max looked into the jaguar's eyes and somehow knew that something special had just happened. Max suddenly felt light on his feet, and his vision had become as sharp as a razor and extremely keen.

The most surprising change was with his hands. When he looked down at his hands, he saw claws coming out of his fingertips. Max quickly waved his arm through air. With the first swoosh, he suddenly felt the quickness, strength, and power that he now possessed in his hands and arms.

Max said, "Thank you for saving my life. I'm forever grateful. Before I leave, you will need to be given a name." Max contemplated for a few minutes and said, "Aha! You shall be named Jinx the spotted ghost."

Max sat with the jaguar for the rest of the afternoon. After a few hours, Max knew the sun would turn into night. His parents expected him be at home before dark. If he did not get home soon, parents would be out looking for him. Especially if they found out that he was not at Cisco Rivera's house playing kickball. He said his goodbyes to Jinx but knew in the back of his mind that this would not be the last time they would come across each other's path. Max flew like the wind back to his house, running faster than he ever had run before.

As Max was coming out of the woods into his backyard, he heard his mother calling for him to come inside for supper. At the supper table that night, Max informed his whole family, especially his brother Robert, that he had found his brother and his friends' secret hidden cave.

Of course, Robert did not believe him and asked Max, "What did the cave look like?"

Without hesitation, Max said, "It was dark and creepy and seemed very deep. I heard a lot of unusual sounds that would echo throughout the cave."

Max declared to his family that he was not scared. Not even a tiny bit scared. Robert still did not believe him, but Max didn't care because he had experienced the most thrilling day of his life.

Chapter Two
Shades of Superpower

MAX KNEW THE DIFFERENCE between right and wrong, good and bad. These morals were taught to him by his parents at a very early age. Even during his pee-wee football days, they called him a "quick cat" because of Max's speed, agility, decision-making, and his football IQ. His high school coach nicknamed him "SC" for "Swift Cat". Max seemed to get out of potential quarterback sacks from opponents' defense every time. Because of Max's speed and agility and the way he read an opponent's defense, he was hard to tackle.

Max was now discovering new and challenging changes in his daily behavior. Looking forward, he set higher expectations for himself. Soon after his encounter with Jinx, Max realized that he had superhuman strength and power. Over the next few years, Max would make A's and B's in school and become an excellent quarterback. He felt in his heart that he was no longer among the normal.

He was walking home from school one day, and he had to stop because his phone was ringing in his backpack. Max reached for his phone. He noticed that it was his mother calling. She let him know that she was going to be about thirty minutes late coming home from work. Max knelt down to put his phone back into his backpack then stood back up.

All of a sudden, Max experienced a strange feeling. He felt as if a sixth sense had come over him. He extended his arm, and at that moment, a baby bird fell into his hand. The baby bird had fallen down about forty-seven feet from a very tall tree. In the blink of an eye, without thinking, as if by instinct, Max climbed up the tree and put the baby bird back into its nest. Max realized that he had climbed up that tall tree so very fast. He realized that he had used a new-found jaguar skill. He looked around to see if anyone noticed what had just happened. He felt all alone. There were no witnesses. No one was around. Max realized that this would become the first of many secret events in his life.

Max and his family took a trip to the local mall to do some shopping for some new back-to-school clothes. They entered the mall and were going to various stores to check on sizes and bargains. For Max, this time was like any other family shopping event.

He had his football in his grasp. Max always had his football with him ever since junior high school.

Max told his parents that he had to use the restroom, and his parents gave him their approval for him to proceed to the restroom. Max went downstairs to the first floor of the mall. This is where the restrooms were located.

Suddenly, Max saw a young man stealing a purse from an elderly woman. The young man started to run away, and Max knew that he had to be stopped. He began following him throughout the mall, dashing in between customers. Max never let this young man out of his line of sight. He noticed that this young man was going to make his exit out of the mall. That was fine with Max because he was already thinking of how he was going to stop him when he exited the mall. Max followed him. After running and chasing him for a few minutes, Max sensed his opportunity to stop the young man. Max cocked his arm back, then *whoosh!* Max threw his football about 150 feet toward the young man. Max had locked onto his target! That football was like a rocket coming out of Max's hand. Bingo! Max succeeded. He was right on target. The football hit the young man right square in the back of the head, stopping him in his tracks.

Max retrieved the elderly woman's purse and his football. He opened his bottle of water and poured it on the young man's face. The young man woke up and complained about being wet, then stood up and attempted to hit Max. Max caught the young man's fist in midair. He twisted the young man's arm, and he fell to his knees, begging for relief. Max's claw had extended when he grabbed the young man's arm. Max told the young man that he could come quietly with him or he could come with his arm in an arm lock to the mall security office. Max silently took the young man by the arm and escorted him back to the mall security office.

He turned the young man over to the security officers at the mall security office. Max told the young man to tell the security officer what he had done. The young man was afraid of Max. He remembered the very painful sting of the grip Max had on his fist. He told the security officer the truth about stealing the elderly lady's purse. Max and a security officer took the purse to the mall lost and found office. Max figured he could find the elderly lady at the mall's lost and found or the security center. He saw the elderly woman writing a statement and approached her. When Max gave the elderly woman's purse back to her, he could tell that her eyes were full of joy and relief. She thanked Max for bringing her purse back to her.

"No problem, ma'am," Max said.

Max thought to himself that it was his duty to get the purse back. Max then went back into the mall to find his parents and brother.

Shea Weathersby was the prettiest girl in Max's school. Shea was also the head cheerleader, the student council president, and the number one volleyball player in the state. Max dreamed about going out on a date with her ever since junior high. Max was Shea's number one fan.

Max stayed late after school to finish up some research on electrolysis for his upcoming science fair project. Max never liked to procrastinate on any of his homework assignments. He was putting the final touches on the research part of his science fair project. All he had to do now was complete the actual testing of all his metals, including copper and aluminum. Max gathered his things into his backpack and headed out of the school library, down the hall to the exit of J. B. Wyatt Senior High School.

Max's usual path was to walk down by J. B. Wyatt Memorial Football Stadium, then cut across to Elm Street for a shortcut to Max's house. As Max was walking by the football stadium, he thought he heard a high-pitched scream coming from underneath the bleachers. Max stopped for a minute. He did not hear anything the second time and began walking again. About thirty seconds later, Max heard that same noise again. This time, Max decided to go investigate the noise. Max went to the gate on the south side of the football stadium. As Max approached the gate, he noticed it was already locked.

Max looked around. There was not another person in sight. He took a great leap and hurled himself over the fence, landing on his feet. He was very surprised and impressed with himself. He realized he had cleared the fence without any extra effort. He refocused. It was time to complete his investigation. He began by looking underneath the bleachers. On the far opposite end of the bleachers, Max saw some shadows. At first, Max could not figure out what he was seeing. He took about twenty-five steps toward the now moving shadows. His keen jaguar eyes started to focus. Now seeing the figures clearly, he knew the shadows were of people. Max was in shock and in disbelief. He saw Tug Johnson and Shea Weathersby.

Tug Johnson was a high school dropout. He always exhibited bad intentions toward girls. Tug did not have a job, and at the age of twenty-two, he was already an alcoholic and frequent drug user. Tug's parents tried to help him with family support, counseling, and rehabilitation. However, Tug had no desire to cooperate, much less participate, in receiving any kind of help.

Tug's parents came home from work one day and Tug had left with all of his belongings. Tug was currently homeless.

Max could tell from a distance that Shea was being held against her will. He knew that he had to do something very quickly or things could get out of control. At that point, Tug had his back turned toward Max, and Max ran as fast as lightning toward Tug. Tug heard something and turned around. Max was about ten yards away from him. Tug was surprised to see Max. Tug thought he had found the perfect place to abduct Shea, but Tug was badly mistaken. Of course, Max had his football. Tug blinked and was about to open his mouth when Max cocked his arm back and threw his football toward Tug.

Bam! Perfect pass.

The football hit Tug directly between the eyes and knocked him unconscious. Max made certain that Tug was no longer a threat to him or Shea. He rushed over to her and untied her as quickly as he could.

If Max had decided to procrastinate, rather than working late to finish his research for the science fair project, Tug would have succeeded with his plan of forcing domestic violence against Shea Weathersby. Shea was very grateful for Max. Shea asked him if there was anything she could do to pay him back for his bravery.

Max thought for a minute and then said, "Will you go to the senior prom with me?"

"Yes, yes, I will!" said Shea excitedly.

So, it was a done deal. Max finally got a date with Shea Weathersby. It was not just an ordinary date. It was a date to the senior prom.

Another time Max noticed his powers was on a cold winter afternoon. Max had gone to Cisco Rivera's house. They threw his football around and studied for an upcoming calculus exam. When Max had arrived at Cisco's house, he noticed two young girls playing outside. One looked to be about four years old, and the other young girl looked to be about two years old. The first thing that went through Max's mind was that neither of the two girls was wearing a coat. The temperature outside that afternoon was in the high twenties, and Max thought being outside without coats in 20-degree weather was ridiculous. Cisco's neighbor's yard always looked like it was in shambles. The weeds were about a foot high, and the leaves had been on the ground for what seemed to be about four years. Interestingly, Max now realized every time he visited Cisco's house, he noticed the two girls were playing outside and their parents were nowhere to be seen. Max knew it was too cold for both of the young girls to be playing outside without a coat, much less to be left unattended by their parents.

Max started walking a direct line to the girl's front door when all of a sudden, he heard the four-year-old scream. Over six years before, the girl's father had started digging a water well. The well was about twenty feet deep and covered with cardboard.

When Max looked over, he knew something terrible had happened. Max only saw the four-year-old standing by the water well, screaming and pointing down to the bottom of the water well. She was yelling her sister's name. Max realized that the younger sister had fallen inside the water well. Max's jaguar instincts kicked into full gear. Without hesitating, Max raced over to the water well. He jumped down into it to retrieve the girl. The water in the well was freezing cold, and it came up about waist-high on her. She was terrified, the water well was pitch-black, and a regular human being could not see anything down that deep in the water well. Luckily for Max, his keen jaguar eyes helped him see, and he located the girl easily.

In a calm and soothing voice, Max said, "Everything's going to be just fine, okay?"

The little girl nodded her head yes.

Max told her that the two of them were going to get out of the well, and the little girl said, "Okay."

As Max was picking her up, he noticed that her right forearm was bent backwards, which probably meant she had broken her arm in the fall. Max looked up with his keen jaguar eyesight and determined that the water well was about twenty feet deep.

Without hesitation, Max took a leap. Boom! Thanks to Max's jaguar leaping ability, both of them were out of the water well.

Cisco and his parents heard the four-year-old screaming, so they ran outside to see what all the commotion was about. By the time they were outside and had figured out what was going on, Max had already saved the girl. Max asked Cisco's mom to call 911 and for Cisco's dad to go ring the doorbell on the little girl's house and inform her parents of what had just occurred. Max let the parents know of the child's broken arm. The little girl's parents did not seem to appreciate Max getting the child out of the well, but Max knew that she probably would not have survived if it were not for him being there at that precise moment. Cisco's parents were considering calling the police and relaying the apparent child endangerment.

Chapter 3
Prom Day

MAY 15TH HAD FINALLY ARRIVED. You may ask what's so important about that day Max had been waiting the last three years of high school for May 15th. It was senior high prom night.

Earlier in the school year, Shea had promised Max that she would be his date for the senior high prom after he saved her from Tug's attack.

Max arrived at Bert's Formal Wear Store to pick up his tuxedo for the dance. Max thought he would be the first customer of the day. He was surprised to see another vehicle already in the parking lot. The vehicle was a 1982 International Scout. It was probably the only International Scout in the county or perhaps the whole state. It was definitely an antique. The person who drove this awesome antique was Allen Caine.

Max and Allen Caine had been friends since the seventh grade when they were paired up in their biology class as lab partners. Allen Caine was considered a nerd by many of his peers at J. B. Wyatt. He wore glasses, had a small build, and was not very muscular.

Allen Caine was a genius. He could read a five-hundred-page book with ease. If you asked him, "What did the second paragraph on page 238 talk about?", he could recite the whole paragraph verbatim. His photographic memory was unbelievable. He was an excellent computer programmer and a wiz at any math subject. He made a perfect score on his college entrance exam. He accomplished this while he was in the eighth grade.

Because of his small build and being a genius, he was an easy target for bullying. Ninety-five percent of the time, Allen Caine was bullied by the jocks of J. B. Wyatt. However, Max Rockafellor and Cisco Rivera were two jocks who actually took up for him.

One day in junior high, Allen was being bullied by some jocks, and Max and Cisco came to his defense. Max and Cisco thought it would be a good idea for Allen to come up with a call sign to let Max and Cisco know when he was in some kind of trouble. He was thinking about a signal when suddenly he had an idea. Allen told both Max and Cisco that he could whistle very loudly. Max and Cisco were very curious. They asked Allen to give them an example of what he could do.

"Okay," Allen said. "But you should cover your ears because my whistle's loud and long!"

Max and Cisco shrugged their shoulders in disbelief. They told Allen to give the whistle his best shot, so that's exactly what Allen set out to accomplish. He put two fingers in his mouth and began to whistle. Max and Cisco could not believe their ears or their eyes. It was baffling that this noise was coming out of such a small individual. Max and Cisco were in shock. They both congratulated Allen on what was now his new call sign.

As Max entered Bert's Formal Wear Store, he said, "Hi, Allen! Dang, I thought I was going to be the first customer here today."

"Nope, SC, you thought wrong!"

They both were excited and anxious to attend their prom. Max of course had his football in hand.

Allen looked at Max and asked, "You are not going to bring that football, right?"

Max said, "Yeah, why not?"

"For one thing..." Allen quickly replied. "...that football is worse than a little infant carrying around their blanket for comfort. You do not want that freaking football to get in the way of you and Shea on this special occasion."

Max thought to himself for a minute. He came to the conclusion that Allen had come up with some good and valid points.

"You're right," Max told Allen. "And I'll leave this football at the house tonight."

"That's a good idea, but I'll believe it when I see it."

"I'll do it, even though it will be difficult for me."

"What time will the limousine be at my house to pick up me and my date?"

"4:30 sharp," Max said.

Max and Allen both received their tuxedos and went their separate ways. They both still had a lot of things to accomplish before the dance.

The limousine first picked up Max, then Cisco, his date, and then Allen and his date. Now they were off to go pick up Shea. On the way to Shea's house, Cisco, Allen, and their dates noticed something that was completely shocking to all of them. Max was without his football. This was the first time any of them could recall that Max did not have his football in his hands. They all congratulated and joked with him about having enough courage to leave his football at his house on this special occasion.

The limousine had stopped, and Max looked out the window and noticed that they were at Shea's house.

Max had a dazed look on his face as he thought to himself, *Could this be real? Could this actually be happening?*

Cisco kicked Max in the leg and said, "Get out and go pick up Shea."

Max opened the door to the limousine, picked up Shea's corsage, and proceeded to the front door. Anxiously, Max rang the doorbell and waited. Suddenly, he stepped back and fell off the porch, messing up the flowers. The door opened, and it was Shea's mother. Max apologized for the squished flowers next to the porch. She asked Max to come in and wait in the parlor. Max noticed two sets of stairs that went up to the second story of Shea's house. He noticed that the floors were marble, and there was some exquisite art hanging on the walls. Max glanced up the stairs, and his jaw dropped to the floor. Shea was at the top of the stairs in a beautiful red dress. Shea started to walk down the stairs to meet Max. Max was trembling. He was very nervous. Shea walked over to him and gave him a hug and a kiss on the cheek. Shea asked Max if her red dress met his standards.

Max responded quickly, "Yes, indeed."

Max took a deep breath and pinned the corsage on Shea. Shea's mother told both of them that they were a beautiful couple. As the beautiful couple headed toward the limousine, Shea's mother stopped them and reminded them to have fun, but most of all respect each other, use common sense and good judgment, and remember the curfew.

They both responded, "Yes, ma'am," and headed toward the limousine.

Now, the three couples were off to enjoy dinner.

While in the limousine, the three couples engaged in some small talk about how they all made preparations for the prom. A few minutes later, they had arrived at their destination: Von Kilmer's Steakhouse. This was the most popular and most expensive restaurant in the county. As the three couples walked through the front doors of Von Kilmer's, the aroma blew them away. They knew at that point that they had picked the right restaurant to have their special dinner.

There were other students of J. B. Wyatt that had also picked Von Kilmer's for dinner. Most of them were jocks.

Midway through dinner, Allen Caine had to go use the restroom. He quietly excused himself from the table and proceeded toward the restroom. Allen was washing his hands when all of a sudden, the restroom door swiftly swung open and hit the wall with a bang. To Allen's surprise, it was the four most obnoxious bullies that attended J. B. Wyatt. The four bullies surrounded Allen.

The leader of the bullies, 300-pound Kong Dong Huey, began his dissertation to Allen, "Dude, it's like this– we need to graduate. You are going to help us graduate. We only need the answer keys to the physics and calculus final exams. You will do this for us and keep your mouth shut!"

Passing the physics and calculus final exams was the only way for the obnoxious bullies to graduate high school and qualify for their athletic scholarships. They were ready to steal and lie to obtain scholarships from various universities for their particular sport.

Just as the four bullies finished talking, Cisco came through the door and asked, "Allen, is everything all right?"

"Everything is A-okay," Allen responded.

Allen and Cisco proceeded back to their table to finish their dinner.

The three couples had finished their main entrée and dessert. They were ready to finally head to prom. As they were leaving the steakhouse, Allen looked back at the four bullies' table. All four of the bullies were giving Allen the evil eye.

The limousine had arrived at J. B. Wyatt. The chauffeur exited the limousine and then went around and opened up the door for the three couples. As they exited the limousine, they saw that there was a red carpet from the edge of the drive all the way to the gymnasium. The parents of the students were on each side of the red carpet, taking pictures as each couple walked. All of the parents were in disbelief when they saw Max walking down the red carpet without his football. You could tell by the smiles on their faces that they were proud of him for leaving his football at home for this special occasion. It was about an hour and a half into the prom when Principal Jack

Croom picked up the microphone. He gathered all the students in front of the stage to get their attention.

"It is now time to give the results of who will be crowned King and Queen of the Senior High Prom!" he announced to them.

Principal Croom asked for the winning envelope for Queen. Anticipation was buzzing throughout the gymnasium. Principal Croom opened up the envelope, looked at the winner's name for a second, and then said, "Your queen for the J. B. Wyatt Senior High School Prom is Shea Weathersby!"

Applause was heard throughout the gymnasium. Then, Principal Croom asked for the King's winning envelope. Anticipation was buzzing throughout the gymnasium. Principal Croom opened up the King's envelope and looked at the winner's name. This time the expression on the principal's face was very surprised. Speculation throughout the gymnasium pointed to the winner being none other than Buck Hamm, the star running back for the football team. He was also Shea's ex-boyfriend and one of the four bullies who tried to force Allen to steal the answer keys for the final exams.

"Your king for the J. B. Wyatt Senior High School Prom is...Max Rockafellor!" Principal Croom announced to the student body.

A hush fell over the room amongst the whole student body, except for Shea, Cisco Rivera, and Allen Caine and their dates who were shouting and jumping up and down and congratulating their new king. Max was in shock himself. He looked at Cisco and Allen and gave both of them high fives and immediately turned around and gave Shea a kiss on the cheek and a giant hug. Cisco looked over at Buck Hamm and grinned, as Cisco could tell that Buck was not overly pleased with the announcement for king.

Max and Shea both went up on stage to receive their crowns and to give speeches to the senior student body. After short speeches by the newly crowned king and queen of the Prom, it was now time for both of them to take their first dance as king and queen. They enjoyed their first dance together.

Things were not going so well for Allen Caine. While the student body was watching the king and queen's first dance, Buck Hamm, Kong Dong Huey, and the other two bullies from earlier at the restaurant had abducted Allen from the gymnasium without anybody noticing.

They took Allen to the second floor of the school. This is where the school library was located. There was a room in the back of the library where all of the answer keys to all of the final exams are stored. Somehow, Buck Hamm, Kong Dong Huey, and the other two bullies found out about the answer keys. They also knew that Allen could unlock the door, which had to be unlocked with a seven-digit push code. Buck Hamm, Kong Dong Huey, and the two bullies thought they could threaten and put so much fear into Allen that he would have no choice but to give them the code to the door.

If they failed exams, it would mean not only would they not graduate in two and a half weeks, but all four of them would lose their athletic scholarships at the universities they had chosen, so it was crucial in the bully's minds to do whatever it takes to get Allen to turn over those answer keys to the final exams.

Kong Dong Huey was growing furious at Allen because he would not give in to his scare tactics. Across from the school library were two wooden doors that led outside to a balcony that overlooked the front of the school. The four bullies decided to take Allen to the balcony. As the boys were walking toward the balcony, the bullies were continuously hitting, kicking, pushing, and verbally abusing Allen. Buck knew how to unlock the wooden double doors that led outside to the balcony. Kong Dong and the other two bullies maintained verbal and physical attacks on Allen. Once Buck unlocked the wooden double doors, he ordered the other three bullies to take Allen to the edge of the balcony.

One last time, the four bullies gave Allen an ultimatum: turn over the answer keys or take a severe punishment.

To the bullies' surprise, Allen showed no fear and absolutely said no to their last ultimatum. At this point, Kong Dong picked Allen up and flipped him upside down so that Allen was hanging over the balcony by his ankles. You would have thought Allen would have been horrified by this, but Allen kept his composure and knew he was about to use his secret weapon on the four bullies.

The whistle. At that precise moment, Allen put his fingers in his mouth and let out a whistle that could be heard across town. Back in the gymnasium, the king and queen had just finished their first dance. The whole student body heard Allen Caine's whistle.

The four bullies became even more furious with Allen and started to vigorously shake him upside down and threatened to drop him. However, Kong Dong knew that he could not do that if he wanted to retrieve the answer keys to the final exams. Back in the gymnasium, Max and Cisco quickly looked at each other and knew instantly that Allen was in some sort of danger. Max and Cisco glanced at their dates and told them that they had to go and they would be back as quickly as they could. Max and Cisco rushed out of the gymnasium and took a look around inside of the high school. They did not see or hear anything that looked out of the ordinary.

At that point, Allen let out another whistle. It came from outside of the high school. Max and Cisco rushed outside the front doors of J. B. Wyatt to investigate where the whistle was coming from. Once they were outside of the school, on the front steps, Allen Caine could see both Max and Cisco while he was hanging upside down. Allen knew he had to give one final whistle to let Max and Cisco know where he was located. After that last whistle, Max and Cisco looked up and saw Allen hanging upside down from the second-story balcony.

In the blink of an eye, Max's demeanor had changed. Max knew he had to do something quickly to save his friend Allen. Cisco could not believe his eyes. He noticed Max's fingertips starting to change and turn into razor sharp claws, and Max's eyes looked as keen as a cat's eyes. There was a tremendous oak tree that was on the front lawn of the school. One of its limbs was as high as the second-story balcony. Buck, Kong Dong, and the other two bullies did not notice that Max and Cisco were below them, so they were unaware that they had been detected. They kept on verbally and physically abusing Allen. Max told Cisco to hold tight and that he was about to resolve this issue very quickly. Max ran over and climbed the tremendous oak tree until he got to first big branch that led over to the balcony. Once Max reached the end of the branch using magnificent and incredible balance, he leapt from the end of the branch to the balcony. The four bullies were in shock. In a matter of seconds, Max first took out Kong Dong, who was holding Allen by the ankles. When Max made contact with Kong Dong, he let go of Allen's ankles and Allen proceeded to fall to the first floor. Max looked down and saw Cisco catch Allen. Max surprised Buck, hitting him so hard that he ended up knocked out, lying in front of the double wooden doors of the balcony. Knowing that Allen was safe, Max proceeded to take out the other three bullies.

Cisco called the local law enforcement to report the incident while Max was taking care of business. As soon as law enforcement arrived, Max, Cisco, and Allen gave their stories of what happened, and law enforcement apprehended the four bullies and escorted them to jail. Allen and Cisco had questions to ask Max because both of them were still stunned about the circumstances of what had just taken place. Max told them that there was a time and a place for this discussion but now was not the time. Max said that it was time to go back into the gymnasium and rejoin their prom dates and enjoy the rest of our prom. Cisco and Allen both agreed with Max.

Chapter Four
College & Draft Day

MAX BROUGHT SUPREME SPEED, agility, power, strength, and keen vision to the football field. Max could run by and run through opposing defenses with ease. When Max ran by the opposing defenders, all they saw was a flash of light going by them. Max was so fast that the defenders usually ran into each other while trying to tackle him.

In terms of agility, Max made the opposing defenders miss tackles because Max could cut, turn, and change direction on a dime. Max just made the opposing defenders look bad.

In terms of power and strength, Max basically used his power and strength to run right over defensive lineman, then the linebackers, and finally the secondary players. Max's arm strength was unbelievable. Max could throw perfect passes to his wide receivers on a rope, and Max's receivers always caught his passes in stride. Even the biggest and toughest defensive linemen and linebackers could not stop Max.

In terms of keen vision, Max could spot holes in the opposing defenses that nobody else could see. Max always took advantage of any opposing defensive mismatch on the football field. Max had learned how to read opposing defenses well beyond his years. Max could spot a blitzing defense, a zone defense, or a man-to-man defense with ease. By learning how to successfully read defenses and having a head coach who trusted Max, he was able to change any play at the line of scrimmage.

College was a very busy time for Max. Between his studies and football, Max's time had to be spent well. Time management was crucial for Max to get everything accomplished on a daily basis. It was a spring morning when Max started his three-mile run. Max ran through campus to the nearby freeway and back to his dorm room.

As Max approached the freeway, he heard about five to seven cracking sounds, and all of a sudden, he looked onto the freeway and saw a tractor trailer start to swerve left and right. Luckily, the big tractor trailer was the only vehicle going north that morning. Up on the hillside, he saw three young men laughing and pointing at the tractor trailer. This was no laughing matter. Max noticed the three young men had rifles in their hands. He knew that he had to get up that hillside and stop them before any more damage could be inflicted. The three young men obviously did not see Max running. As he approached, he observed all three young men were reloading their rifles. They were ready to cause some more damage.

Max's jaguar instincts took effect. His eyes were focused on the three young men, and his fingertips turned into razor sharp claws. He started running fast toward them and took a huge leap. Before Max could reach the three young men, they took aim at another tractor trailer. Max pounced on all three young men at once, clawing each one of them on the face and arms. The three young men had to be stopped. The men did not see Max coming. Max vanished on the other side of the hill before they could tell who or what attacked them. All three of them were screaming in pain. The truck driver had pulled over to check on his tractor trailer when he heard them screaming for help. The truck driver ran up the hill and saw them and their rifles. He called 911 immediately. Within a matter of minute, an ambulance, fire truck, police cruiser, along with about four television crews had arrived on the scene. The three young men were transported to a nearby hospital, treated for their wounds, and released into police custody. That night on the local news, it was reported that some large cat attacked the three young men who tried to cause havoc on the local freeway. This was the first time that Max actually used his claws to stop someone.

In college, Max earned the nation's top honors for a quarterback for four straight years. Max helped his team win a national championship in four consecutive years. And now, fourteen years after his special encounter with Jinx, whom he got all his special powers from, Max had a chance to fulfill his dreams and be selected in the first round of the Continental State Football League (CSFL) Draft. Football meant the world to Max. Not only did he enjoy the game, but he liked being around his teammates and coaches. Football provided Max with a mental toughness that he could use in everyday life and a respect for the game of football.

It was a cool brisk Saturday morning in the windy city of Chicago. If you were a fan of pro football, excitement was in the air because this day was the beginning of the CSFL Draft. The whole Rockafellor clan was on hand to see Max get drafted. Max had been projected by the pro football analysts and scouts to be the number one pick in the draft. The San Antonio Rattlers had the number one pick in the draft. The draft war room of the San Antonio Rattlers had leaked out some information that they were going to use the first pick on George Taft, a defensive end from Alabama A&M. The owner of the San Antonio Rattlers was Wyndham Firestonne, a billionaire by inheritance. Simply put, everything Mr. Firestonne received was basically given to him without an ounce of his own blood, sweat, and tears.

Wyndham Firestonne said that he would like to get some depth on the defensive side of the Rattlers. The truth was that he needed more skilled players on both offense and defense. However, over the past four years, Mr. Firestonne had selected a quarterback in the first round. Because all four quarterbacks had failed miserably to develop, Mr. Firestonne had received some intense backlash and unfavorable feedback from the media based on the last four consecutive drafts. Mr. Firestonne really wanted the national and local media to get off his back and leave him alone.

Mr. Firestonne had once said he wished that Max Rockafellor would have skipped his senior year of football and entered the draft as a junior. Mr. Firestonne was furious when Max decided to stay for his senior season. Mr. Firestonne referred Max a "selfish player". Some of the national and local media agreed with Mr. Firestonne, but the majority of the media thought that Mr. Firestonne was cuckoo.

Max clearly stated at the end of his junior year in college that he intended to come back to the University of Arkansas and lead the Razorbacks to a fourth straight national championship. Max had told the media that he could wait one more year. He not only wanted to play football, but he also wanted to earn and receive his degree in Accounting and Finance. Max's Grandmother Huff always told him that a degree was one thing that nobody could ever take away from him. Max also wanted to set the example for underclassmen and to let them know that the game of football should be cherished by any player, coach, and fan. A college football player had only four years of eligibility to play college football or any other sport in college athletics. Max always said people should enjoy their college experience while they could.

Max knew when he turned pro and started to earn his paycheck to play professional football that it was more than just a game. Pro football was a business and a full-time job.

In early September, the buzz around the CSFL was that Max Rockafellor would be the first pick and that George Taft would be the second pick. That all changed one week prior to the CSFL draft. Mr. Firestonne supposedly said that he wanted his first pick to be on the defensive side of the ball.

There was one person on the staff of the San Antonio Rattlers that was up in arms about this whole situation: the head coach, Forrest Morgan. You see, Coach Morgan was headstrong with a fiery temper, and he had a nose for knowing a top prospect when he saw one. Coach Morgan disagreed with Mr. Firestonne. Four years before, Coach Morgan wanted to pick an offensive lineman with the first pick. He got a quarterback. The second year, he wanted to pick a running back. He got a quarterback. The third year, he wanted a wide receiver. He got a quarterback. The last year, Coach Morgan wanted a linebacker. Once again, he was overruled by Mr. Firestonne. He got a quarterback. Coach Morgan had been coaching football for over thirty-five years, and that was at all levels: high school, college, and professional football.

Coach Morgan had seen quarterbacks come and go; he had coached some great quarterbacks and some awful quarterbacks throughout his career. Coach Morgan knew that the San Antonio Rattlers could not pass up on Max Rockafellor because he was a franchise quarterback.

One of the rules of the CSFL was that once a team made a selection in the draft, that selection could not be changed. So, if a coach, general manager, or owner made a selection that other members of the franchise disagreed with it, it was too bad. That draft pick was a done deal. Coach Morgan fully understood this rule, and he knew that somehow he had to convince the San Antonio Rattlers General Manager Theodorre Forsythe, a complete "yes man" to Mr. Firestonne, to make Max Rockafellor San Antonio's number one pick.

The almighty dollar ruled the CSFL, just like any other big business in the United States of America. As Coach Morgan was thinking of how to convince GM Forsythe to make the correct pick, all of a sudden, a brilliant scenario popped into his mind. He quickly called GM Forsythe on the phone and told him that he had some urgent information to pass along to him. Coach explained to his boss that he needed to stop by his hotel suite as quickly as possible.

It was ten minutes after midnight. The draft was only nine hours away. Coach Morgan knew his meeting with GM Forsythe would have to be quick and to the point about the decision to draft Max Rockafellor. Coach had been pacing back and forth in his hotel suite for about forty-five minutes, trying to wait patiently for GM Forsythe. He remembered that his dad would always tell him, even at an early age, "patience is a virtue". He was about to second-guess his dad on that quote.

Suddenly, there was a loud *bam, bam, bam* on the door. Coach Morgan answered the door, and finally GM Forsythe had arrived. Coach Morgan quickly pulled GM Forsythe inside and began explaining to him why Max Rockafellor should be San Antonio's number one draft pick. GM Forsythe listened, but he still insisted that San Antonio would be better off picking George Taft instead of Max Rockafellor.

Coach Morgan knew that he was down to his last straw. He believed GM Forsythe cared more for the almighty dollar than he did about the coaching staff or even the players. At that point, Coach was very angry. He reminded GM Forsythe that a local survey concluded that should San Antonio draft Max Rockafellor, his jersey would sell more than any other player in the CFSL draft.

Further, Coach blurted out, "The San Antonio Rattler's merchandise store phones would be ringing off the hook with fans trying to purchase his jersey!

Not just fans from Texas, but football fans from all around the United States. Internet sales would sky-rocket, not only this year but for years to follow!"

GM Forsythe's eyes started to gleam with dollar signs. Coach knew right then he had won over his general manager.

As the time ticked closer to the opening of the CSFL draft, Max Rockafellor was a cool, calm, collected cat. He was waiting backstage with his family and other hopeful draftees and their families.

Everybody has that one friend that is obnoxious, loud, and always thinks that they should be at the center of attention. That friend for Max Rockafellor was Franzo Chandler. He was the class clown in high school as well as college. Even though he was big enough to play defensive end or offensive tackle, Franzo did not play football. All Franzo wanted to do was be the team water boy. All the families that were backstage became a little bit happier and less nervous when Franzo started making everyone laugh with his off-the-wall jokes that never made any sense.

It was now about ten minutes from the start of the CSFL draft, and there was some new uneasiness in the San Antonio Rattler draft war room. Coaches and staff members were hearing that Mr. Firestonne was downstairs confirming to the national and local media that the San Antonio Rattlers would make George Taft, not Max Rockafellor, their number one pick in the year's draft. News of the

George Taft pick quickly made its way backstage.

Once the Taft family heard this news, they all began boasting and started to be very obnoxious, especially to the Rockafellor family.

Olivia Pendergrass was Max's sports agent. She had swagger, style, and confidence. Many of the male sports agents wished they could be like her. She had outstanding skills in evaluating talent, and she knew how to tease and use her female qualities to help sway owners to give her clients the most lucrative contract in any sport. She was also backstage with the Rockafellor family.

Olivia stood up from the Rockafellor table and made her way over to the Taft table and said something that was only heard by the Taft family, but it was short, sweet and to the point. All the Taft family turned very quiet except for George Taft who was acting like a childish three-year-old. Olivia was the person who put a stop to the ridiculous and outrageous behavior.

All of a sudden, everybody in the entire arena heard the theme music from the CSFL, and the commissioner of the CSFL, William Q. Picard, was heading to the podium to begin the year's draft. As Commissioner Picard was given the card for the San Antonio Rattlers' first pick, George Taft stood up and started walking very confidently to the edge of the stage.

Everyone in the arena went silent, and Commissioner Picard said, "With the first pick of the CSFL draft, the San Antonio Rattlers select...Max Rock-afellor from the University of Arkansas."

The crowd in the arena went ballistic.

Suddenly, George Taft fell to his knees and started throwing a temper tantrum, showing off his immaturity.

The crowd started chanting, "SC, SC, SC!"

There it was– the nickname that was given to him by his high school coach. Max's family was elated and joyous, knowing that their loved one was se-lected first overall in the year's CSFL draft. Max was very humble, shocked, and surprised that his name was just called out by Commissioner Picard.

Meanwhile, the Taft family was trying to console George backstage, but it did not take long for George Taft to hear his name called because he was the second pick selected in the draft going to the Denver Stallions.

Mr. Firestonne was outside of the arena, puffing on a cigar, when several journalists from the lo-cal and national media approached him and asked why he changed his mind from Taft to Rockafel-lor. One of the journalists asked why any organiza-tion would use their first pick on a quarterback five straight years. Mr. Firestonne's face instantly turned bright red, and smoke was coming out of his ears. Everyone could tell that he was furious. Mr. Fires-tonne instantly picked up his cellphone and called GM Forsythe to get some questions answered.

Meanwhile, Max was celebrating with his family and friends backstage. A loud whistle came from Franzo Chandler. Max asked Franzo what the whistle was for.

Franzo turned to him and said, "Turn around and look over there at the most gorgeous and beautiful woman that has ever walked this earth."

Max turned around and was amazed by this stunning brunette woman walking towards him. She introduced herself to Max, saying, "Hello, Mr. Rockafellor. My name is Madison Mayfield, and I am a television reporter and anchor for KAJTV channel 77 in San Antonio. Do you mind if we have a quick interview concerning your number one pick in this year's CSFL draft?"

For the first time in Max Rockafellor's life, he was speechless.

Franzo leaned in toward Max and said, "You need to start talking to this fine Georgia peach before she gets away. If you don't, I'll find a way to be her water boy."

Suddenly, Max came out of his bashful trance and started giving his interview to Ms. Madison Mayfield.

Ms. Mayfield began, "So, Max, have you ever been to San Antonio, Texas before?"

"Yes, many times," Max answered. "My brother Robert has lived in the New Braunfels-San Antonio area for several years now."

Max told her that he enjoyed all the theme and water parks, Alamo, and the beach, which was just about two hours away. The interview took only about twenty minutes. Once the interview was over, Max asked Ms. Mayfield if they could go out for dinner at a future date.

Ms. Mayfield turned around and politely said, "Why, of course! Who wouldn't want to go out with San Antonio's most eligible bachelor?"

With a gleam in his eye, Max quickly went over to his family and gave them thanks for all of the support that they had given him throughout his childhood and teenage years. Max did not get say thank you or goodbye to everybody because the San Antonio Rattlers entourage quickly pulled him away to head to the airport and get on the Rattlers' private jet so they could head back to San Antonio and introduce him to the staff, teammates, and fans of the Rattlers.

The next couple of weeks were going to be very hectic and fast for Max. He would be learning a new play book, trying to earn the other players' trust and respect, and most of all, proving to Coach Morgan that he was right by picking him as the number one player in the draft.

Max only thought he knew how to handle the media. Being a professional football player was definitely different from being an amateur. Each day after practice, there was a member of the media from each of the fifty American states and territories, plus seven from international countries including Mongolia.

After a couple of weeks, Max learned reporters were interested in his playing abilities on the field. Some reporters were just interested in trying to start rumors and mischief. When there was a particular reporter trying to start mischief, Ms. Mayfield would always come to Max's rescue.

Ms. Mayfield had been following Max's professional life for three months. She was ready for Max to act on the promised dinner and a night out on the town that he made back in Chicago. Immediately after the interview was over, Ms. Mayfield confronted Max about the dinner. Max started to blush and apologized about the lack of respect he was showing her and promised that the next Friday night, he would repay her with a dinner and a night on the town.

Chapter Five
Reunited

COACH MORGAN WAS IMPRESSED with how fast Max was learning the playbook. It was a warm June afternoon the last day of mini-camp. Coach wanted to make sure some of the new plays he added for the offense the previous off-season would produce positive yardage against the league's number one defense. On this day, Coach had the number one offense and number one defense execute these new plays. The offense was shredding apart the defense with the new plays. Two of the Rattlers' top defensive players, Rocco "The Gambler" Izzo and Brutus "The Pancake" Willis, had decided that enough was enough.

They were going to welcome Max, the new star rookie quarterback, to the CSFL. Both Rocco and Brutus knew Coach Morgan's rule about not making contact with the quarterbacks during mini-camp. However, they both wanted to introduce themselves to Max with maximum authority. On the very next play from scrimmage, Rocco and Brutus simultaneously rushed and blitzed toward Max with a full head of steam and crushed Max into the turf of the Rattlers Stadium. As Coach Morgan blew his whistle and ran closer to Max, he anticipated that his star quarterback was hurt. Coach Morgan did a quick 180-degree turn, scolded his star veteran defensive players, and sent them to go run the bleachers of the Rattlers Stadium.

Max's longtime friend Cisco "Titan" Rivera helped Max to the sideline quickly so that the trainer for the San Antonio Rattlers, Romero "Doc" Garcia, could check out the injury before taking Max into the training room for further examination.

Max was favoring his non-throwing arm and left shoulder. Coach Morgan hoped that Max's injury was not serious. Max was lucky to have Romero as his athletic trainer. You see, Romero Garcia had been a trainer for fifty-three years. Doc started his occupation as an athletic trainer at the age of eighteen. Along the way, he picked up some valuable tricks. In most cases, he helped his players get completely healed from their injuries and ready game day. Doc's experience had made him the best athletic trainer in the CSFL.

As Max and Doc were headed back to the training room, Doc promised Max that he would get him back on the playing field in no time at all. Max knew by the look he saw on Doc's face that Doc was genuine in his words.

It had been two hours since Max had entered the training room. During that time, Rocco and Brutus came by to apologize to Max, and he accepted the apologies.

Max had noticed that Doc had been pacing back and forth, and something either seemed to be bothering Doc or he just wanted to find some information about Max. Max broke the ice by asking Doc if he had ever watched or followed him during his college football career.

"Well, by golly, SC," Doc responded. "When the local sports station was broadcasting your team, I never missed a minute watching you play. You were incredible...I mean, fantastic! Max, you always amazed me with your smart, quick decisions, arm strength, passing accuracy, and above all your quickness on your feet! SC, how did you ever get so quick?"

"Well, Doc, I don't know," Max replied. "Guess I was just born with that natural ability."

Max did not want to reveal to Doc what really happened to make him so quick. He quickly realized that Doc was a smart cookie when it came to figuring out how to solve some difficult puzzles. Doc was probing and prodding Max with some hard questions. Doc told SC that there had been some strange things happening there at the stadium over the past year.

"It started about nine months before you were drafted by the San Antonio Rattlers," he said.

SC had a startled look in his eyes and said, "Like what?"

"Well, SC, come see my little hideout underneath Rattlers Stadium," Doc beckoned.

The entrance of Doc's hideout was a hidden trap door in the back of the training room. It led to some stairs that went far beneath Rattlers Stadium. The stairs going down were not well-lit. When SC and Doc reached the bottom of the stairs, Doc flipped a switch. SC could not believe his eyes. For what he saw, this was a huge control center Doc had manufactured. The first thing SC thought was that this could look like what the top brass at the Pentagon would use if there were ever a national or world crisis in the making.

Doc told SC that he had been working on this hideout for several years. However, he ramped up its progress when he "found this particular cat".

SC looked confused and said, "A cat made you finish this hideout?"

Doc smiled and said, "This was not your ordinary house cat."

Doc told SC that on a Sunday night the previous fall, the San Antonio Rattlers had just beat the L. A. Lightning. It was a brutal game. The quarterback for the San Antonio Rattlers played an awful game, and if it were not for Rocco and

Brutus, the Rattlers would have lost the game.

With 1:17 left in the game, Brutus sacked the L. A. quarterback. Before the quarterback's knee touched the ground, he fumbled the ball. Rocco was in the right spot at the right time. He scooped up the football and went eighty-seven yards for the touchdown.

There were several players on both San Antonio and L. A. that were hurt after that game. Doc stayed at the stadium until about 4:25 a.m. to make sure that all of the Rattlers' hurt players were able to get into playable condition.

"The last player left the stadium about 3:30 a.m. I had locked my part of the stadium. As I was walking to my vehicle, suddenly out of the corner of my eye, I saw a flash of light, and I felt a gust of wind go right past me. I glanced back toward Rattlers Stadium, and I saw something like a shadow near the edge of the stadium. Curiosity got the best of me. So, I walked over to see what this thing or creature was. I slowly walked closer, and the creature let out a loud hiss. At that moment, I realized it was some sort of huge cat.

"I stayed near the cat for about twenty minutes. Then I turned and started walking back to the part of the stadium that was near my office. And while I was walking to unlock the stadium, this cat followed my every step. I led this cat down to my hideout. I offered it food and water.

"As I turned on the lights, the cat looked at your poster and started going crazy. I thought to myself that you and this cat had some sort of weird chemistry or connection going on. Then when the San Antonio Rattlers drafted you, I knew that I would be able to put the pieces of this tough puzzle together."

At that moment, Doc turned around and pointed to a corner of the hideout and said, "That cat, that Jaguar!"

SC was in disbelief and stunned as he walked closer to the jaguar. He recognized that it was Jinx, the "spotted ghost" that saved his life fifteen years earlier.

Right then, Doc saw the connection between SC and Jinx. Jinx leapt toward SC, put his front paws on him, and started licking his face.

"This is as calm as I have ever seen Jinx," Doc told SC. "Is there anything else you care to explain or inform me about you two?"

After the shock of seeing Jinx dissipated, looking around at the magnificent control center Doc had built, SC said, "Yes, Doc. Something happened about fifteen years ago."

SC proceeded to tell Doc about the relationship between him and Jinx. After SC was finished with his story, Jinx was actually sitting in SC's lap and purring like a little kitten.

Without SC realizing, Doc had walked behind SC and poked his arm with a needle. When SC felt the needle, he let out a scream.

"What are you doing?" he yelled at Doc.

At the same time, Jinx let out a wicked hiss toward Doc.

Doc told SC and Jinx to settle down. He explained that he was only verifying his hypothesis.

Doc noticed the color of SC's blood was not red. Now, Doc knew his hypothesis was correct: both SC and Jinx had blue blood.

This was actually not really shocking to Doc because he had already studied SC's medical records. These records revealed that SC had not been sick for fifteen years.

Earlier that month, Doc was lucky enough to retrieve a blood sample from Jinx. He was able to accomplish this feat without getting injured or killed by Jinx. Once Doc got a sample of Jinx's blood in a vile, he did some extensive tests on it. As it turned out, Jinx had a high concentration of Vitamin C in his system. Animals can produce their own Vitamin C. This helps the animals in fighting off different viruses, diseases, and sicknesses.

Now Doc understood one of the reasons that SC had not been sick over the last fifteen years. Doc felt that this was the perfect time to tell SC why he decided to build this so-called control center.

Doc informed SC that the crime in San Antonio and surrounding areas had become rampant over the last couple of years, and he thought that some, but not all, of the local San Antonio police force was corrupt. Doc proceeded to tell Max he thought that Max was the one person who could bring justice back to San Antonio and the surrounding areas.

Doc flipped an electric switch on the massive control board, and across the room, a light shone down onto a round-looking cabinet. Its doors opened, and to Max's disbelief, he saw what appeared to be a superhero suit hanging up. Doc explained to Max that this was a special suit. Max put the suit on. It was not as heavy as he expected.

Max already had a very good sense of balance. However, with the unique tail on the suit, his sense of balance was even greater. Max's eyes seemed to be almost bionic. Max could zero in on a small breadcrumb laying in a corner four hundred yards away.

Another surprise was his hearing. Max heard some grumbling from up above the Jag-Man control center. He could actually hear Coach Morgan getting upset because he could not find Max or Doc. At that point, all Max could do was laugh.

Doc threw a binder at Max. He knew that Max would go into a self-defense mode. Max did actually go into a martial arts stance, and he swiped away the binder. Doc reached down picked up the binder. It was fully shredded.

"How do you like your new claws?" Doc asked Max.

"I am amazed!" Max said.

Another light turned on. Max glanced over, and he saw some accessories that he really liked. There was a Jag-Truck, Jag-Cycle, Jag-Four-Wheeler, Jag-Helicopter, and a Jag-Boat.

Max was speechless for a while. Doc walked Max over to these accessories and showed him each one. He explained how they all worked. Max thought about how he could use the special gadgets. He visualized using each one to help him catch all the bad guys and gals.

So, after it was all said and done, Mr. Garcia asked Max one simple question: "Max, are you the one that I can count on to bring the criminals and villains of San Antonio to justice?"

"Yes, Doc," Max responded. "I will be your Jag-Man."

Doc grinned from ear to ear and said, "From me and all the law-abiding citizens of San Antonio, we thank you and salute you!"

At that point, Max looked down at his watch. He could not believe how late it was. He told Doc that he had to hurry up and leave because he had to get ready for a dinner date with Ms. Mayfield.

Doc laughed and said, "That Ms. Mayfield is beautiful. Now, get along and make sure you treat her like the lady that she is. And you stay out of trouble."

Max rushed through the secret passage of the Jag-Lair, went through the training room, and on to his vehicle. On the way back to his condo, Max phoned Lennigan's Tavern on the Green. This was an upscale bistro in San Antonio. Max made sure that the reservation that he had made earlier in the week was still good. Max received the verification that he was looking for and proceeded to his condo.

One good thing about having Jag blood in you is that it makes you a quicker than the average human being. It took no time at all for Max to get ready for his dinner date. He was almost done. He had to put the finishing touches on his hair with the help of just a little bit of Dapper Dan.

As Max settled into his sports car, he glanced down at his watch to see how he was doing on time. To his surprise, he was a little bit ahead of schedule.

Max had found out from a few acquaintances that Ms. Mayfield adored flowers that were in the color of lavender. On the way to Ms. Mayfield's residence, Max stopped by a respected florist in San Antonio and picked up a dozen lavender roses.

As usual, Max was punctual. As a young boy, Max's parents instilled in him that it was very important to always be punctual. Max had reached the doorstep with lavender roses in hand. He leaned over to ring the doorbell.

As the door opened, Max glanced up and thought to himself that Ms. Mayfield looked like a beauty queen. Ms. Mayfield thought to herself that Max looked like a polished gentleman. They exchanged greetings, and Max extended his hand with the lavender roses to Ms. Mayfield.

"How did you know that lavender was my favorite?" Ms. Mayfield asked Max.

"A little bird told me," Max responded.

They stepped inside Ms. Mayfield's house so Ms. Mayfield could get her purse and keys. After a little small talk, the couple left for Lennigan's Tavern on the Green.

This was Ms. Mayfield's favorite place to feast on some fine cuisine. After they pulled up to the covered driveway, both doors were opened for them, and Max handed over his keys to the valet. As they walked into the bistro, they were quickly shown to their own quiet, secluded corner of the dining room.

They both glanced over the wine list and then selected a wine, hors d'oeuvres, and their main course. Over the course of dinner, they gave each other little overviews of their childhoods, teenage years, and, of course, college lives.

During dinner, Max noticed that two of the waiters were giving him and Ms. Mayfield the evil eye. Max casually engaged in conversation with her about local crime rates in San Antonio.

"Well, Max, crime in San Antonio has skyrocketed over the last decade, and there was one person solely responsible, Poncho Guerrow. Poncho and his thugs have wreaked havoc on the city of San Antonio and its citizens. There are rumors running around San Antonio that Poncho Guerrow has infiltrated the police force and the city council."

"Has anyone tried to put a halt to Poncho Guerrow's shenanigans?" Max responded.

Ms. Mayfield said, "Yes, many have tried. But every time someone tries to stop him, bad things happen to them. Poncho threatens their family members. So the people trying to put him behind bars just essentially gave up."

Then Ms. Mayfield pointed out, "I just wish that there was one person in San Antonio who would finally show some bravery and act as a leader and bring Poncho and his band of thugs to justice."

As Ms. Mayfield finished talking, Max noticed that the two waiters were acting a little strangely. Max asked Ms. Mayfield politely if they could find dessert elsewhere. She was a little disappointed because Lennigan's served the best homemade chocolate and coconut cream pies in San Antonio, probably the best in the whole state of Texas, but she quickly got over her sadness.

She quietly told Max that getting dessert somewhere else was fine with her.

The two mischievous waiters noticed that Max and Ms. Mayfield were getting close to leaving and rushed over to their table. Each one was carrying a tray, and each tray had a single cup of coffee on it. With crazy-looking smirks on their faces, they told Max and Ms. Mayfield that these mocha lattes were "house compliments" of the owner.

Ms. Mayfield was about to indulge in her cup of coffee when Max quickly took it away from her hand and said "Sorry, honey, we have to leave this very minute."

Amazed by what had just happened, all Ms. Mayfield could say was "Okay."

The two waiters were in a state of shock. One of them said, "How can you disrespect the owner of this fine establishment and not drink his own special blend of mocha latte?"

"Maybe next time," Max said. "Right now is not a good time for us. And besides, I only drink coffee in the morning."

Max took Ms. Mayfield to a local bakery establishment several miles down the road to finish their dessert and earlier conversation. Max told Ms. Mayfield that he thought there could be some changes concerning law and order with respect to his new city of residence.

"Really?" Ms. Mayfield asked. "Exactly what will happen?"

"Do not worry, honey. I just have a keen instinct!"

After they had finished their dessert and conversation, Max drove Ms. Mayfield back to her townhouse. Ms. Mayfield told Max that she had a lovely time and she hoped that there would be many more to follow.

Max was blushing and said, "Yes, ma'am. Yes, indeed."

Chapter Six
Rouge Stone Valley

EARLY THE NEXT MORNING, Max showed up at the Jag-Lair, eager to learn and test his new equipment. When Max entered the Jag-Lair, he noticed that Doc was already there analyzing some graphs and going over some statistics on crime in San Antonio. Doc told Max that in the past three years, the population and size of San Antonio and surrounding areas had risen by fourteen percent. And with the population rising, the local crime rate also rose by twenty-three percent. Max asked Doc what the main reason for the population increase of San Antonio was.

Doc replied with one word: "Rouge stone!"

Doc began giving Max some insight on rouge stone and the effects it was having on the local communities and economy. Doc told Max that sixteen miles south of San Antonio, there was a suburb of San Antonio called Rouge Stone Valley. Rouge Stone Valley was the number one place in the United States of America where rouge stone could be located. It was also the first time that oil had taken a backseat to anything in Texas in 147 years.

People had arrived in Rouge Stone Valley from every state in the United States and from every corner of the world trying to strike it rich with rouge stone. Doc told Max that there were some rumors going around that the current and reigning villain of San Antonio area, Poncho Guerrow, had been threatening, stealing, and forcing people out of Rouge Stone Valley, making the citizens and miners sell their mining rights over to him, and forcing the Rouge Stone miners to mine for him and only him. Doc told Max that Poncho Guerrow was one bad apple.

Doc said that Rouge Stone Valley should be the land of opportunity, not the land ruled by a dictator. Max asked Doc if he had ever crossed paths with Poncho Guerrow. Doc said yes, one time. There was some land on the south side of San Antonio which philanthropist Jason Locksmith had donated and granted to a local charity group that helped abandoned special needs youth.

This land was going to be used to build a school, small library, gym, theater, cafeteria, and dormitories to help these young adults with special needs. But after Jason Locksmith passed away, Poncho Guerrow came up with fraudulent documents stating that John Locksmith had sold this land to Poncho Guerrow. Doc said he saw Poncho Guerrow at a city council meeting and proceeded to give him a piece of his mind about the situation. The next thing he knew, Poncho Guerrow blew cigar smoke from his cigar into his face and pushed him down, and his bodyguards kicked him as they walked past him. Max said surely other citizens or public officials, or police officers saw what took place. Doc agreed, saying the citizens, public officials, and police officers did see what happened, but the citizens were too scared to say anything, and the public officials and police officers were already bought off by Poncho Guerrow.

"That's a low-down, dirty shame," said Max.

He told Doc maybe him being drafted by the San Antonio Rattlers was a miracle. Max said that the man upstairs may have brought him here to San Antonio to bring back law and order. Doc told Max that it would be very nice to have some law and order brought back to the city of San Antonio. All of a sudden, Max had an idea, and he shared the idea with Doc.

Max told Doc that he was going to get with his agent Ms. Olivia Pendergrass and Coach Forrest Morgan, General Manager Theodorre Forsythe, and the San Antonio Rattler organization and tell them that he wanted to make an appearance at Rouge Stone Valley so he could sign autographs for the hard-working miners free of charge. This would also enable Max to view Rouge Stone Valley during the daylight, and he could also try and get a sense of the morale of the miners. Doc told Max that was a magnificent idea and to leave the Jag-Lair immediately and go start putting his plan into action.

After talking to Ms. Pendergrass and the Rattler organization, they both agreed that Max's idea would be an awesome P. R. move for both Max and the Rattler organization. After Max left the meeting with Ms. Pendergrass and the Rattler organization, he gave Ms. Mayfield a call to let her know about what was going to happen. Max told her that she was the first news reporter to know and that she could have the first interview with him.

Later that afternoon, Ms. Mayfield showed up at the San Antonio Rattler headquarters to conduct a breaking news broadcast and interview with Max about the Rouge Stone Valley free autograph signing day. Max said in the interview that he wanted to give back to the community of Rouge Stone Valley and their hard-working miners by giving them a chance to receive a free autograph from the new rookie quarterback of the San Antonio Rattlers. He also told Ms. Mayfield that he hoped he could get in touch with the lead foreman of the Rouge Stone Valley Mine so he could get a tour of the mines and see how they were running and operated on a daily basis.

The day had arrived for Max to go to Rouge Stone Valley to sign his autographs for the miners who were San Antonio Rattlers fans. As Max, Ms. Pendergrass, Coach Forrest Morgan, and General Manager Theodorre Forsythe entered Rouge Stone Valley, they saw many signs telling Max and the San Antonio Rattler organization thank you for coming and seeing them. The citizens of Rouge Stone Valley were very appreciative and honored to have them in their community.

Max was told that the Rattlers fans camped out all night the previous night so they could be one of the first ones in line. The line started to form around 5 a.m. so they could get their free autograph. But there was one person who was not so excited to see Max or the Rattler organization in Rouge Stone Valley, and that was Lex Cruz, who was the lead foreman of the Rouge Stone Valley mining operation. He was handpicked by Poncho Guerrow to oversee the mining operation of Rouge Stone Valley. Cruz was in his mid-50s, a former military general whose personality consisted of being a harsh, vulgar, intolerant, older individual. The citizens of Rouge Stone Valley could not stand him, especially the miners.

As Max exited the Rattler limousine, he was welcomed to the chants of "SC! SC! SC! SC!"

Max was ushered to the table where he was going to sign his autographs. Ms. Mayfield and

Patrick C. Moore

her camera crew were there on site and told that Max judging by how long the line with Rattler fans was, she thought he may wind up with writer's cramp after it was said and done.

Max responded back to MS. Mayfield that it was okay and that the fans deserved all the autographs he could hand out.

Lex Cruz, on the other hand, was not enthused by what he considered shenanigans. He told Max and the San Antonio Rattler organization that they were wasting his time and the miner's time with all this nonsense, and that he wanted the Rattler organization to pay a dear price for the amount of time being missed by the miners not mining. Max was finished signing autographs, which totaled to over 1,300. One of the cool things Max did after he signed his autograph for the fan was that he was able to give about three to five minutes with each fan to get to know them on a personal level and would also take a personal photograph with each fan.

Now, Max was ready to take a personal tour of the Rouge Stone Mine. It would take about two and a half hours to complete the tour. As Max was touring the mine, he noticed that the expressions on the miners' faces were very gloomy, sad, and unenthused about trying to find that rare precious metal rouge stone. Max could tell when Lex Cruz looked at one of the miners that the miner looked scared and intimidated by him. Cruz received a text and told Max that he had to go back to the corporate office to take care of some business that needed his urgent attention.

Max was relieved because now he'd be able to interact with some of the miners to get a sense of what was really happening behind the scenes of the Rouge Stone Mine. Max looked over and saw one of the miners, who appeared to be about eighteen years old. Max went over to him and tried to start a conversation with him.

"How are you?" asked Max. "What is your name?"

The teenager looked scared, but Max could recognize that he wanted to say something.

Finally, the teenager said, "Hello, Mr. Rockafellor. My name is Rubio Mars."

He told Max that he had been working in the mines for about nine months. Max asked Rubio if he enjoyed working at the mine. Rubio said he did at first, but when Poncho Guerrow made him and his family sign over their family's mining rights to him and then Lex Cruz was made the lead foreman, everything went downhill from there.

Rubio Mars went on to tell Max that over sixty-five percent of the safety procedures were abolished by Cruz and the working hours and shifts were changed from eight-hour shifts to twelve-hour shifts; they also went from working five days a week to working seven days a week with no overtime or compensatory time being awarded to the miners. Rubio also told Max that if any of the miners found any rouge stone, they had to turn it over to Lex Cruz and that the miner would only receive one and a half percent of the rouge stone instead of the full hundred percent if they had still owned the mining rights.

Max had a disgusted look on his face. Max could not believe that these miners were being so mistreated and abused. Max was thinking silently, and he knew that he had to put an end to this corruption. Then Rubio told Max that the worst part was if any of the miners found any rouge stone and did not report it to Lex Cruz and they were caught, a severe and devastating punishment that would be carried out on the miner. Rubio went on to say that he heard rumors of a makeshift dungeon that was deep inside the Rouge Stone Mine; this was where the miners who did not report and were considered stealing the rare precious metal rouge stone were severely tortured.

Max asked Rubio if he had ever seen this makeshift dungeon. Rubio said he had just heard rumors about the dungeon from other miners. Max gave Rubio some moral support and told him to keep the faith and that things would turn around for the better very soon, not just for him, but for all the miners in Rouge Stone Valley.

At that point, Max heard a man with a very deep and harsh voice yelling and screaming. Max realized that this person was yelling and screaming at Rubio.

This person said in a very upset voice, "Rubio, you were told in the morning briefing not to have any social contact with the visitors. You have disobeyed the orders and now will be severely punished for this violation."

It was Cruz. He was about two feet from Rubio, and he raised his hand and was about to backhand Rubio right across his face. Max was in shock about how how quickly the situation has escalated. Before Lex Cruz could make contact with Rubio's face, Max caught Cruz's hand. Cruz was now even more furious. He yelled and screamed at Max.

"What are you doing?! You have no right to interfere with any kind of punishment or discipline that is handed out here!"

"Yes, I can," responded Max. "When I can clearly see abuse to a miner being carried out by supposedly a superior with no sense of judgment."

Cruz informed Max that his tour of the mine had just finished, and Max was escorted out of the mine. Max did not have a chance to say goodbye to Rubio and prayed for Rubio's safety and wellbeing.

Max had to return to the San Antonio Rattlers practice facility to prepare for his first professional football game being held in three days. Practice had been closed for all of the summer workouts and leading up for two-a-days. There were leaked reports saying that Max Rockafellor and his receivers were in sync since about the first week Max had arrived in San Antonio.

After practice, Max entered the Jag-Lair and gave Doc a full report on what he discovered at the Rouge Stone Valley Mine. Doc was not surprised at anything that Max had reported and was in full agreement that Poncho Guerrow and Lex Cruz had to be stopped immediately.

For the next three days, Max was very busy and engaged between practicing for his first professional football game and gathering intelligence reports and doing some major research with Doc, trying to figure out the best way to resolve the current and dangerous situation going on at Rouge Stone. Doc informed Max that his intel revealed that every Sunday night, Poncho Guerrow and his cronies gathered at his upscale estate at Rouge Stone Valley to participate in illegal poker games.

Doc said all the key personnel in Poncho Guerrow's regime participated except for Lex Cruz. Doc said he could not find out why or where Lex Cruz was going during these illegal Sunday night poker games. Max had an idea where Lex Cruz was. He reminded Doc that Rubio Mars told him that there was a secret dungeon Poncho Guerrow had created to torture any of the miners who had disobeyed his rules and regulations.

Doc and Max were starting to put a game plan together; they decided that the first order of business was to find this secret dungeon, put an end to the torture, and free any miners who were being held hostage against their will. Then they would give reassurance to all the miners that Max came in contact with that everything was about to change for the better for all of them. Next was to locate and find Poncho Guerrow's estate, finally meet Poncho Guerrow face-to-face, and make him understand that his days of putting fear into the citizens of San Antonio were coming to an abrupt end.

Doc suggested to Max that Jinx should go along with him when he went to Rouge Stone Valley, and Max excitedly agreed. Max told Doc that Jinx would be a major asset in stopping the corruption at Rouge Stone Valley Mine.

Sunday had arrived. It was finally time for Max Rockafellor to show why Coach Forrest Morgan and the San Antonio Rattlers drafted Max number one overall.

Tailgating started early that morning around 6 a.m. for the noon football game between the San Antonio Rattlers and the Miami Tiger Sharks. Miami was the heavy favorite coming into the game. Max was excited and ready to play some football. The Tiger Sharks defensive players had been talking a lot of smack and rhetoric toward Max, saying that he was going to set the record among rookie quarterbacks for having the most sacks in a rookie's first game.

Max just shrugged off all those comments and told reporters that his actions would be shown on the playing field. For a rookie quarterback, Max was cool, calm, and collected. The joke was on the Tiger Sharks defensive squad. Max shredded the Tiger

Sharks with 381 yards passing, four passing touchdowns, 122 rushing yards, and two rushing touchdowns. Max spread the football around to six different wide receivers, tight ends and running backs.

The Tiger Sharks soon realized why Max Rockafellor was called "swift cat" in college. Max led the San Antonio Rattlers to a 46-0 shutout victory over the heralded Miami Tiger Sharks. This was the first shutout for the San Antonio Rattlers in eleven years. As the game was ending, Max went across the field to shake hands with the Tiger Sharks. All of the Tiger Sharks defensive squad went up to Max and congratulated him on a well-executed game plan. All of them told him that they were impressed with his power, agility, and speed.

As Max was coming off the football field, there were many reporters trying to get his attention for his first post-game interview. He noticed Ms. Mayfield in the back getting pushed around by other reporters. Max headed straight to her.

Finally, he reached Ms. Mayfield and asked her, "Ma'am, would you like to be the first reporter to receive my first post-game interview?"

"Why, yes, Mr. Swift Cat!" she replied. "I would love to be the first reporter to receive your first post-game interview."

The first thing Ms. Mayfield did was congratulate Max for being named the player of the game. Max was surprised by this announcement but was grateful.

He told Ms. Mayfield that he was glad to have his first professional game completed and he was excited by the results. After a few more questions, Max told Ms. Mayfield that it was time for him to leave and go celebrate with his teammates in the locker room.

As Max entered the locker room, the first two players to come up and congratulate him were none other than Rocco "The Gambler" Izzo and Brutus "Pancake" Willis. They both told Max that their preconceived notions of Max were dead wrong and that they questioned his abilities while in practice but when game time came along, "SC" took it to a whole different level.

They both were extremely pleased and even though this was the first game of the season, they both felt like they were both playing on a potential playoff team. Rocco and Brutus had been playing in the CSFL for seven years and had never been to the playoffs. Both Rocco and Brutus told Max that they both were rejuvenated and excited to be playing winning football.

At that time, Coach Forrest Morgan let out a loud whistle to get all the players' attention. Coach Morgan stood up on a chair and told the players to look around and seize this moment.

"Look at each other's faces and the excitement and pride that everybody has," he said. "If you do not want to lose this exciting and joyous feeling, then you have to work even harder. Listen to your position coaches and have each other's backs on and off the football field. If y'all want to be a championship football team, then each and every day you must put in extra effort and go the extra mile to be successful. So, enjoy this victory tonight and tomorrow, but be ready to come back to work Tuesday and go full throttle. Take it one game at a time. This is the first game of a sixteen regular-game season."

Coach Forrest Morgan then called Max to the center of the room.

"Now, what do y'all think about your new rookie quarterback? Can he play some football or what?"

Max's teammates started shouting and chanting, "SC! SC! SC!" as Coach Forrest Morgan began to look around the locker room. This is what he had envisioned when he decided to draft Max.

As Max finished getting cleaned up, showered, and changed into his civilian attire, he knew it was time to head down to the Jag-Lair and get ready to put an end to Poncho Guerrow's rule over Rouge Stone Valley.

Max entered the Jag-Lair and met an extremely happy and excited Doc Garcia.

"Wow, wow, wow!" Doc yelled out. "Man, the San Antonio Rattlers fans have not seen that kind of quarterback play in decades. SC, you were magnificent and outstanding!"

Max thanked Doc for the deserved compliments and told Doc that games like that would be the standard for the San Antonio Rattlers.

With that said, Doc started to explain to Max his research and ideas on how to take down Poncho Guerrow at Rouge Stone Valley. Doc restated that the dungeon was the number one priority and told Max that he found an entry point in the mine that Max and Jinx could enter unnoticed. Then he showed Max how far the distance was between Rouge Stone Valley Mine and Poncho Guerrow's mansion, which Doc estimated to be about eleven miles. Doc said his research showed that the living quarters of the butler, maid, and groundskeeper had a long hallway attached to the mansion and using this entryway would give Max and Jinx the best opportunity of entering Poncho Guerrow's mansion undetected.

Max took in all of this information as he started getting ready to start his quest. Doc said that he made some minor adjustments to his and Jinx's suits and that they were ready to be worn. Doc also reminded Max about the special features on the Jag-Mobile, saying that especially the stealth mode should be used upon entering Rouge Stone Valley and leaving the Rouge Stone Mine heading towards Poncho Guerrow's estate.

"If you have any problems," said Doc. "I will be watching you from the satellite and will try and help you if anything out of the ordinary arises."

The sun had set over the southern part of Texas, and it was now time to start the mission: (SRV) Save Rouge Stone Valley. Max and Jinx were in their suits, ready for action. Last-minute details were studied.

Max looked at Doc and said, "I think we are ready."

Doc told Max– or "Jag-Man"– "It is time to rock and roll."

Jag-Man looked over at Jinx and asked him, "Are you ready to put an end to the crime and corruption at Rouge Stone Valley?"

Jinx let out a very loud and taunting hiss, sprinted over to the Jag-Mobile, and jumped in. Jag-Man gave Doc a thumbs up and a fist pump, and then he was off to the Jag-Mobile.

While Jag-Man and Jinx were traveling toward Rouge Stone Valley, Doc came over the radio system to let Jag-Man know that he had sent an encrypted e-mail to some loyal and trusted law enforcement and to Ms. Mayfield, giving them both detailed information about the corruption that was about to be stopped. It also detailed an approximate time of when they both should arrive. Jag-Man asked Doc how he came up with such an exact timeframe. Doc said he used advanced math equations based on several variables that would affect how long he thought it would take Jag-Man and Jinx to complete the mission depending on how many obstacles they could endure until the mission was complete. Doc basically said it was just my instinctive hypothesis. Jag-Man told him he hoped his educated guess was spot-on accurate.

Doc noticed that Jag-Man was about four miles from Rouge Stone Valley and advised

Jag-Man to go ahead and move into stealth mode in the Jag-Mobile. Jag-Man agreed and flipped the control switches to convert to stealth mode. Jag-Man told Doc that Jinx even looked surprised by this new technology.

As Jag-Man and Jinx were getting closer to Rouge Stone Valley, Jag-Man caught himself hoping that Rubio Mars was safe and sound. Jag-Man and Jinx arrived and cruised through Rouge Stone Valley all the way to the Rouge Stone Valley Mine without being detected using the stealth mode on the Jag-Mobile.

Jag-Man and Jinx arrived at the mine and exited the Jag-Mobile, looking for the alternative entrance that Doc told Jag-Man about earlier in the week. It did not take long for Jag-Man and Jinx to find the alternative entrance.

Once inside, Jag-Man had to use the built-in flashlight on the arm of his suit to help see the pathway to the dungeon, which was long and curvy and pitch-black. Without using a flashlight, it would be very difficult, even with his keen jaguar eyesight. It took them about two hours and forty-five minutes to find the dungeon. Jag-Man was not surprised that the dungeon was that deep into the mine because if Lex Cruz were torturing the innocent miners, Lex probably wanted the dungeon to be deep enough into the mine so the miners being tortured could not be heard. Out of sight, out of mind.

As Jag-Man and Jinx approached the entrance to the dungeon, they were about five hundred yards from the entrance, and Jinx stopped suddenly and gave out a small but sincere hiss.

Jag-Man looked down at Jinx and asked Jinx, "What is the matter, lil' buddy?"

Then Jinx put his right leg out and pointed down. Jag-Man used his flashlight and shone it in the direction that Jinx was pointing to, and lo and behold, there was a tremendous hole in the ground that looked about twenty feet deep and as wide as the narrow corridor.

Jag-Man shone his light down into the hole to get a better look. They both were in for a big and scary surprise. They both were in awe because they came to realize that there must have been about 3,000 rattle snakes in the bottom of that snake pit.

Both Jag-Man and Jinx jumped back about five feet when they processed in their minds what they were actually looking at: a freaking snake pit. Then quickly came the eerie sound of all 3,000 rattle snakes using their rattlers at the same time. Jag-Man told Jinx that if any of the miners tried to use this route as an escape route, they would be doomed.

Jag-Man and Jinx looked at each other, and they knew what they had to do. Each of them took about ten steps backwards then started sprinting forward, and when they reached the edge of the twenty-foot-deep snake pit, they both leapt into the air and jumped across the snake pit. They both landed about seven feet on the other side of the snake pit.

Jag-Man swiped his brow and told Jinx, "Let's keep moving forward toward the dungeon entrance."

About two hundred yards from the dungeon entrance, Jag-Man turned off his flashlight. He just relied on his keen jaguar vision to make their way to the entrance of the dungeon.

Jag-Man noticed that were about five guards armed with small machine guns protecting the entry point of the dungeon. Jag-Man and Jinx quickly moved toward the guards and took them out before they knew what had happened. Jag-Man destroyed their radios and unloaded their weapons before they went any further.

Jag-Man opened the door and soon realized that there was definitely a dungeon in the mine because the door led to a spiraling staircase, which looked like it never ended. Quietly and urgently, both Jag-Man and Jinx started down the spiraling staircase. This dungeon had to be about two and a half stories below the mine. Once they reached the bottom, they were both surprised that there were not any guards at the bottom of the spiraling staircase.

Max guessed that Lex was confident enough that intruders would not make it past the rattler snake pit, and even if they did, they would have to go through the five guards he had posted at the top of the spiraling stairwell. Jag-Man and Jinx started to map out and visualize how they were going to put their plan into action.

Jag-Man noticed that Lex had installed several Middle Ages torture devices in the dungeon. Jag-Man saw a lead sprinkler, torture coffin, brazen bull, neck torture, a chair of torture, a thumbscrew, a rack, and a tongue tearer. The lead sprinkler was usually filled with molten lead, tar, boiling water, or boiling oil, and it was used to torture victims by dripping the contents onto different body parts.

The coffin torture method involved placing the victim inside a metal cage roughly the size of a human body– hence the name. The brazen bull was a solid piece of brass and was cast with a door on the side that could be opened and latched shut. The victim would be placed inside the bull, and a fire would be set underneath it until the metal would become literally yellow as it was heated. The victim would be slowly roasted to death while screaming in amazing pain.

The neck torture was humiliating and painful; this punishment was something of an endurance test where the victim would be hooked into the neck device, either made of metal or wood, which prevented the victim from adjusting into a comfortable position.

The thumbscrew was designed to slowly crush fingers or toes, but larger devices were also used to crush elbows and knees. The rack was designed to dislocate every joint of the victim's body. This torture device was made out of a wooden frame with two ropes fixed to the bottom and the other two into the handle on top.

The tongue tearer looked like an oversized pair of scissors. It could effortlessly cut the victim's tongue. The chair of torture was a terrible, intimidating torture device. The chair was layered with five hundred to fifteen hundred spikes on every surface with tight straps to restrain its victim and was made of iron. It was used to get confessions out of victims. Jag-Man noticed that all the Middle Ages torture equipment was being used except for the brazen bull.

There were about thirty-five guards and Lex carrying out these torture techniques on innocent miners. Jag-Man did not see or hear Rubio, and that was unsettling to him. All of a sudden, Jag-Man heard Lex yelling and shouting at all of his guards to circle around the brazen bull. Lex asked two of the guards if the victim had been properly placed into the brazen bull.

They both answered back creepily with "Yes, sir."

Lex told his guards that this was the first time the brazen bull would be used on their disloyal miners. Jag-Man looked around at the other torture victims and could see the fear in their eyes at knowing that something horrible was about to happen. Lex approached the brazen bull and tapped on the side of it. With a crazy laugh, he asked the victim if they were sorry for what they did. There was no answer from the victim.

Then Lex said, "Since you will not beg for forgiveness and for your disloyalty, I have no choice but to unleash this brazen bull as you bellow out pathetic screams and slowly roast to death! You should never mess with an ex-general of the Army, and you should have never spoken to that sorry, losing quarterback of the San Antonio Rattlers!"

"What the heck?" Jag-Man said to himself. "That is Rubio Mars inside of that brazen bull."

At that moment, Lex told the two guards to set fire underneath the brazen bull, and Lex was laughing along with an evil smile. Jag-Man started to hear Rubio Mars screaming in pain as the brazen bull started to get hotter and hotter. Jag-Man knew that there was no time to waste. If he was going to save Rubio Mars from the brazen bull, the time to act was now.

Jag-Man glanced over at Jinx and said, "Now is the time to go into battle. Let's stop these criminals once and for all."

The battle was on. Jag-Man and Jinx rushed swiftly into the dungeon quickly taking out the guards one at a time. This was indeed a skilled attack on the criminals inside the dungeon. Within minutes, half of the guards had been defeated.

Rubio's screams were getting louder and louder, and Jag-Man knew there was no more time to waste. As Jinx was fighting off the remaining guards, Jag-Man went straight toward the brazen bull. At the same time, Lex realized what Jag-Man was going to do and rushed over to try and stop him, but Jag-Man had a special dart to give to Lex. In the sides of Jag-Man's boots, there were darts that could paralyze a person temporarily.

All Jag-Man had to do was kick Lex in the sternum, and this would activate the darts from Jag-Man's boots. Just as Jag-Man expected, Lex was running with a full head of steam toward Jag-Man, and just when Lex was about five feet away, Jag-Man leapt into the air and with a mighty kick to the sternum, a dart ejected from Jag-Man's boot and connected right on target to Lex's chest, paralyzing Lex instantly. This would keep him down for about forty-five minutes.

After being reassured that Lex was temporarily paralyzed, Jag-Man quickly put out the fire underneath the brazen bull and pulled Rubio out of it and into safety. Rubio was in shock, and Jag-Man did all the buddy care techniques he had learned to good use on him. Then Jag-Man went over and helped Jinx take care of the guards who were still standing and putting up a fight.

Once they were taken care of, Jag-Man went to each victim who was in a torture device and set them free and then started to apply self-aid and buddy care to all of them. They were all very thankful to Jag-Man and Jinx. Jag-Man immediately called Doc to tell him that paramedics needed to be sent to the Rouge Stone Mine because Rubio had been severely burned and the other miners needed urgent medical care. Doc said he would get right on that. Phase one of mission SRV was complete, and Jag-Man and Jinx were about to enter phase two.

Doc told Jag-Man to proceed with mission SRV. But, before Jag-Man and Jinx left the dungeon, Jag-Man decided to give Lex Cruz a dose of his own medicine and strapped Lex Cruz into the chair of torture until law enforcement arrived to take him off to prison.

Jag-Man also recommended that the rest of the miners stay in the dungeon until law enforcement arrived and to take care of Rubio Mars; he reinforced to them that they should not go up the stairs and attempt to go out of the mine that way unless they wanted to fall into a snake pit of about 3,000 rattle snakes; they all seemed to agree with Jag-Man.

Earlier, Jag-Man had noticed that one of the guards came out of a secret passage to enter the dungeon. Jag-Man found that guard who was severely punished by Jag-Man and Jinx and asked him if that secret passage would lead him to Poncho's mansion. The guard would not answer, so Jag-Man gave him an ultimatum: either tell him the truth or he was going to set Jinx into full jaguar mode or let the miners take him up the stairs and lead him to the rattle snake pit and throw him over into it. Jinx let out a huge hiss. That changed the guard's mind very quickly, and he verified that the secret passage would indeed lead Jag-Man and Jinx to Poncho's mansion.

Jag-Man looked at Jinx and said it was time to rock and roll into phase 2 of mission SRV. Jag-Man and Jinx exited the dungeon and entered the secret passage that led to Poncho. Fortunately, there were no obstacles until they reached Poncho's mansion. That was because all of the main figureheads were busy with their games inside.

The so-called game hall was on the third floor of the mansion. There was some slight resistance that Jag-Man and Jinx encountered but nothing they could not handle with accurate and swift precision. Once they made it to the game hall, Jag-Man noticed that there were two tables with twelve people sitting at each one. Two spots were empty at each table, and those four people were at the bar getting more intoxicated.

So, there was a total of twenty-four people that Jag-Man and Jinx had to put in theirplace. Poncho was sitting at the head of one table, laughing at how he was taking advantage of these poor miners. Jag-Man overheard Poncho tell the men who were sitting at his table that Lex should have contacted him by now to let him know that the brazen bull was a success. Jag-Man could tell the look on Poncho's face was one of concern that he had not been contacted by Lex yet.

Jag-Man had all the Poncho boasting that he could take. Jag-Man gave Jinx a wink, and they barged into the game hall unexpectedly. Like on the football field, Jag-Man was quickly taking care of business along with his friend Jinx. It helped that Poncho and most of his friends were very intoxicated. As Jag-Man and Jinx were fighting the other bad guys, Jag-Man glanced up and saw that Poncho was going to try to escape.

Jag-Man quickly disposed of the thug he was currently entangled with, ran across the room, lunged toward Poncho, and tackled him. Jag-Man wrestled with Poncho until he basically tapped out. Then Jag-Man called Jinx to stand guard over Poncho until he could get ahold of Doc to let him know that phase two of mission SRV was complete. He and Jinx were as good as rouge stone.

Jag-Man told Doc that he needed his assistance with trying to find evidence of the fraudulent mining papers that Poncho had forged. With the new technology that he had invented, it did not take long for Doc to find the hidden safe that was located in the game hall; once Jag-Man found the hidden safe and opened it up, he had all the evidence he needed to convict Poncho and all of his acquaintances.

Doc told Jag-Man that law enforcement, Ms. Mayfield, and the paramedics should be arriving at Poncho's mansion within the next five minutes. Jag-Man looked down at Poncho, who was tied up, and told him that his reign of terror, fear, and pain toward the citizens of Rouge Stone Valley, San Antonio, and the greater suburbs was over.

"Not a chance!" said Poncho. "You may have got me this time, but not you or anybody else will stop me for long. I will be back, meaner and tougher than ever. You can count on that! By the way, who are you?"

"I am Jag-Man," he said. "The inquisitor of the night."

In moments, law enforcement had arrived. Ms. Mayfield, news crews, and the paramedics also arrived at Poncho's mansion, ready to serve justice and due diligence, reporting the news and providing healthcare to the miners. Jag-Man and Jinx returned to the Jag-Lair unnoticed, celebrating with Doc that mission SRV was a success.

Jag-Man has one last message:

Listen up, my good friends. You know the difference between right and wrong, good and evil. When you see something that is not right, something that is wrong or evil, stop what's happening right in its tracks. Until next time, my good friends, keep your jag-eyes wide open and jag-instincts sharp.

About the Author

Patrick C. Moore was born in 1969, in the Magnificent Land of Opportunity and Natural State of Arkansas. He grew up in North Little Rock and Pine Bluff. Growing up he was intrigued with Superheroes and this fascination led to his interest into researching stories related to Superheroes. Mr. Moore is a retired veteran of the Arkansas Air National Guard. 189th Air Lift Wing, 189th Logistics Readiness Squadron. The Military taught him to have a definiteness of purpose, have a burning desire, and take action. Jag-Man shows Max how to do what is right even when nobody is looking-- to have faith, gratitude, and stand by his morals. The Epic Tale of Jag-Man is Mr. Moore's first book.

J. Kenkade
PUBLISHING®

Our Motto
"Transforming Life Stories"

Also Available from J. Kenkade Publishing

ISBN: 978-1-944486-55-6
Visit www.amazon.com
Author: Garrett Cottrell

In this dystopian novel, a group of teens with superhuman strength find out through a group of Hunters that they must either go on the run to survive or be forced to go to camps set aside for "Abnormals." They decide to go on the run and train in their newly found powers. They gain friends and lose friends along the way, but they fight well together.

Also Available from
J. Kenkade Publishing

ISBN: 978-1-944486-87-7
Visit www.amazon.com
Author: Margaret Joanne Rice

All who hear tales of Madam MaRooska's world-renowned yet exclusive specialty resort at Bellingfast Estates clamor to be granted attendance every year. One of the most compelling events in this two-week excursion is an elaborate masquerade ball in which guests can disappear into the personas of any historical figures they wish. However, Constance Stallings knows firsthand just how quickly this game of illusions can turn nefarious. Born into wealth and privilege but determined to make a name for herself as an author, she embarks on a second trip to Bellingfast with her family in the hopes of finishing her novel, The Angel Doll, and perhaps even uncovering the tragic mystery that looms over her last encounter with the seemingly cursed estate.

Also Available from
J. Kenkade Publishing

ISBN: 978-1-944486-93-8
Visit www.amazon.com
Author: Margaret Joanne Rice

Set in the Old South after the Civil War— specifically on a tobacco plantation in Staunton, Virginia— this story revolves around three key groups of people. Plantation owners, plantation workers, and Native Americans play integral roles in this saga. They often intersect and prove necessary for each other to exist in their sociopolitical climate. The conflict in the story involves an ancient Indian folktale about a baby skull hidden on plantation property in a grandfather clock that is shrouded in superstition. This skull is said to have magical powers, and when it disappears, many strange events begin to unfold.

Also Available from
J. Kenkade Publishing

ISBN: 978-1-944486-88-4
Visit www.amazon.com
Authors: Marshall B. Crowder and Luz Eneida Torres

The Wanderer's Enduring Love is a love story that spans centuries. Beginning in the 18th century with Lusamba and Marcelo. A young couple full of life and love that get torn apart by the brutal transatlantic slave trade. In a second attempt at love, Lusamba tries again with Elias, only to be horrifically denied. Modern day couple Neida and Marcel meet on a dating site and immediately realize that they have too much in common for their meeting to be merely coincidental. They decide to explore any connections they might have through DNA testing and soon discover that they have a shared past. Are they prepared for what they might discover? How are they connected? Will what they find bring them closer or tear them apart? Follow them and travel to Cameroon, Puerto Rico, California, Georgia, and Arkansas. See how they use modern technology to uncover the past and discover their future.